9-98

# MOUSE

Balloons

LANDMARK EDITIONS, INC.

P.O. Box 270169 • 1402 Kansas Avenue • Kansas City, Missouri 64127
(816) 241-4919

# SURPRISE

Written and illustrated by
Alexandra Whitney

Dedicated to:
Gram, Grandma Jeanne, and Grandpa Ed,
because they love me and I love them.
To Mama and Mi Mi
for all their help.
And to Spice, my mouse who died —
I know Spice would like this book very much.

COPYRIGHT © 1997 BY ALEXANDRA WHITNEY

International Standard Book Number: 0-933849-64-8 (LIB.BDG.)

Library of Congress Cataloging-in-Publication Data
Whitney, Alexandra, 1987-
    Mouse surprise / written and illustrated by Alexandra Whitney.
    p.  cm.
    Summary:  A kitchen full of mice try not to wake the cat as they scurry
about making a big surprise for the feared feline.  Includes the recipe for
the cat cake.
ISBN 0-933849-64-8 (lib.bdg. : alk. paper)
 1. Children's writings, American.
[1. Mice—Fiction.        2. Baking—Fiction.
 3. Children's writings.     4. Children's art.]

I. Title.
PZ7.W61155Mo     1997
[E]—dc21
                                    97-18803
                                    CIP
                                    AC

Creative Coordinator:  David Melton
Editorial Coordinator:  Nancy R. Thatch
Production Assistant:   Brian Hubbard

Printed in the United States of America

Landmark Editions, Inc.
P.O. Box 270169
1402 Kansas Avenue
Kansas City, Missouri 64127
(816) 241-4919

# MOUSE SURPRISE

This is a delightful book that young children and adults, too, can enjoy for hours. There are so many exciting and interesting things to see on every page. You can have a wonderful time, not just reading the story, but letting your children tell you all of the many activities they see happening, scene by scene, and mouse by mouse.

Alexandra Whitney has a vivid imagination, and she is an extraordinarily skilled artist. If I asked her to draw twenty mice, each one doing a different thing, I am sure that in a matter of minutes, she would draw twenty mice, each one doing a different thing. If I then asked her to draw twenty more mice doing twenty more different things, she would proceed to draw twenty more mice doing twenty more different things.

I have no idea how many times she could keep on adding twenty more mice without duplicating the activities of some of them. But I think it might be hundreds, perhaps a cast of thousands, because Alexandra has the kind of inventive artistic mind that seems to know no boundaries. It simply goes on and on.

Alexandra usually carries a sketchpad with her, and if she has nothing else to do, she immediately opens that pad and starts to draw. Some people may think she loves to draw because she is so good at it. But I suspect the opposite is true. I think she is so good at drawing because she loves to do it.

She also is a wonderful inventor of comic situations. The story is an example of her exceptional creativity. It is told with a great deal of cleverness and humor.

Alexandra is a quiet little girl. In all the time I worked with her, I don't think she said more than two hundred words to me. But she always listened very carefully, which I liked. She is very friendly and eager to please. And I love to be pleased!

Now — it's early morning, time for Alexandra Whitney's mice to wake up and start to prepare their big surprise.

You should turn the page quickly, so you won't miss the ring of the opening bell!

— David Melton
Creative Coordinator
Landmark Editions, Inc.

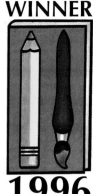

**WINNER**

**1996**
**WRITTEN &**
**ILLUSTRATED**
**BY... AWARD**

Ding! Dong!  Andrew rings the bell.  "Wake up," he calls.
"Today we make the big surprise!"

Katie turns off her alarm.  Sam is sleepy and hides
under the covers.  Matilda does her morning exercises.
Rosa wakes up Tony with a horn and a loudspeaker.

6

Fern looks in her red book. She will need it today.

Marco brushes his teeth. Jerome always sings in the shower. Many feet patter down the stairs and up the ladder.

Ebony turns on her light. "Come on, everybody!" she says. "Let's get started!"

Everyone is so excited! Molly, Polly, and Dolly ride on
top of the measuring cup. Dolly laughs and kicks up her heels.
Bill and Bob carry the butter under the hot-air balloon.
Emily drives the truck. Kenya uses the loudspeaker.
"Let's go faster!" she tells everyone.

8

Satsuki makes the crane lift up an egg. Jean waves a
flag and helps pull the cart. "Here comes the milk," she says.
Jamal rides by on a buzzing bee.

Fern stands on the salt shaker. "Shhhh!" she says.
"Everyone must be quiet or we will wake up. . . *you know who!*"

The crane and the car are too noisy! We turn off their
motors. We have to push and pull everything — *very quietly.*
*We do not whisper. We do not cough. We do not sneeze.*
We must be careful and not wake up — THE CAT!
That would spoil our plans for the big surprise.

10

Caleb pulls the cart of lemon drops all by himself.

But most of the other things are too heavy. We have to work together in teams to move those.

Laurie tries to hypnotize the cat. "You are still very sleepy," she says again and again.

Whew!  We got past the cat!  We are so happy!
Some of us put on a circus show on the rim of the bowl.
"Stop doing that!" Fern warns.  "You might fall off!"
Zack is a wonderful pilot.  He brings the other egg.
Amelia flies the helicopter.  She wants to help, too.

Ben and Sally discover that lemon drops are really sour.
Ivy wants a bite of licorice.  Rex is acting silly.  He has fun
pouring salt on Rita.

Tamika loves the taste and the smell of vanilla!

Tyler skateboards over to help the others untie the egg.

Fern stands on a high shelf. She still has the red book. So she tells everyone what to do.

"Stop playing in the sugar!" she orders. "We will need all of it to make the surprise!"

Ollie uses a vacuum sweeper to spray sugar into the bowl.

14

Jed jumps up and down on the scissors. When the strings are cut, the butter will plop into the bowl.

Susie waves the signal flags. So Amelia drops rocks from the helicopter to break the eggshell. Omar scuba-dives in the milk. Baby Sara wants some milk in her bottle.

Oh, no!  The cat is awake!   It is time for her lunch!
We have to hide in a hurry!
Some of us jump into the bowl of batter.  Others hide
behind the cabinet door.  Some of us climb into drawers.
Fern tries to hide behind her red book.

16

Three of us hide behind the bowl of almonds. Some of us squeeze between books or crawl inside of cups. All of us are very, very quiet. We do not move or make a sound.

Emma acts like she is the Statue of Liberty. She stands very still so the cat will not see her.

We are lucky!  The cat did not see us.  She finally leaves.
Now we can get the other dry ingredients.  Lester and
Lucy pull buckets of flour up by ropes.  Bill and Bob sprinkle
salt from the hot-air balloon.  Some of us get ready to add
the baking powder.  Others throw flourballs at each other.

18

Fern climbs up the bowl with her red book. Marsha finds cranking the hand mixer is hard work. Mike gets a free ride in the electric mixer. Spinning around makes him dizzy!

Some of us go swimming in the batter! Oh, no! Morris cannot swim! Debbie throws a lifesaver to him just in time.

19

Fern looks in her book and says, "Time to butter the pan."
This is our favorite part!
*Wheeeeeeeeeee!*  We love to slide on the butter.
Whoops!   Victor and Jenny crash into each other.
Ahmed falls down.  Peg skates by on two pats of butter.

20

Patty sings with a boom box. Carlos applauds. Maria dances the hula. Karen and Aaron dance together.

Angela wears a *Super Mouse* cape. She sure slides fast! Some of us eat ice cream cones. They taste so good! "Come on! Let's dust the pan with flour," calls Fern.

21

Satsuki sounds the horn and lowers the crane. The big
pitcher tips over and the batter pours out.
    The batter smells. . . *WONDERFUL!*
    When Fern looks the other way, some of us jump into
the pan. We gobble down some batter. *Yum! Yum!*

Fern sets the timer. "Everyone be careful!" she warns. "The oven is very hot!"

Some of us wear heat-suits. In case there is a fire, Joe and Janet are ready with the water hoses.

Soon the cake is done. We take it out and let it cool.

Fern still has her red book. Look! It is a cookbook! It tells her what to do.

"Spread the chocolate frosting evenly," she reads aloud. We scoop up the frosting and spread it over the cake. "Now we get to decorate the cake," says Fern.

24

Cindy delivers licorice on a hook. Jim and Hilda hammer the gumdrops into place. Gabby is a sneaky one. She nibbles on a gumdrop. Alma climbs up a red licorice rope with lemon drops on her back. Oops! Ed is stuck in the frosting!

The cake is finally finished. Now the surprise is ready!

"SURPRISE!" everyone yells. "HAPPY BIRTHDAY, CAT!"
The cat is so excited! She loves the surprise!
Our band marches in and starts to play.
Everyone sings Happy Birthday and dances about.
We toss confetti into the air and let go of our balloons.

26

Hurray! Our good friend Alex comes to the party, too!

Now comes the best part.
We all get to help the cat eat the cake!
 And it is SCRUMPTIOUS!

For safety, be sure to let a grownup watch you make your cake.

## ALEXANDRA'S CAT CAKE RECIPE

MIXING AND BAKING

1. Heat the oven to 350 degrees.

2. Use one 8-inch round pan and one 4-inch round pan.

3. Grease both pans with oil and dust them with flour.

4. Sift the dry ingredients into a mixing bowl:
   - 2 Cups of Flour
   - 3 1/2 Teaspoons of Baking Powder
   - 1 Teaspoon of Salt

5. Mix the following ingredients in another bowl:
   First cream together:
   - 1 1/2 Cups of Sugar
   - 1/2 Cup of Soft Butter or Margarine

   Then add to the mixture and blend well:
   - 2 Eggs (Beaten)
   - 1 Cup of Milk
   - 1 Teaspoon of Vanilla

6. Gradually stir the dry ingredients into the wet ingredients and blend the combined mixture really well.

7. Now use an electric mixer on medium speed to get the batter all nice and fluffy.

8. Pour the batter into the pans. Fill them up about half way.

9. Then put both pans in the oven.

10. Bake for 20 to 30 minutes.

11. When the cakes are done, remove the pans from the oven.
    Hint:
    Cake is done when a toothpick stuck into the center of it comes out clean.

12. Let the cakes cool completely.
    Then remove them from their pans.

Do not use a sharp knife or pointed scissors

## FROSTING AND DECORATING

Use a ready-made chocolate frosting or mix up your own recipe.

1. For the cat's face —
   use the big round cake.

2. For the cat's ears —
   cut two big triangles out of the small cake. Stick them onto the big cake, using a bit of the chocolate frosting.

3. Now spread the frosting all over the tops and sides of the cat's face and ears.

4. For the inside of the cat's ears —
   use 2 red gumdrops.

5. For the cat's eyes —
   use 2 lemon drops.

6. For the cat's eye pupils —
   put a tiny bit of chocolate frosting in the middle of each eye.

7. For the cat's nose —
   use 1 red gumdrop.

8. For the cat's mouth —
   use a curved strip of red licorice.

9. For the cat's whiskers —
   use three black licorice strips on each side of the cat's nose. Put a short strip of licorice from the nose to the mouth.

10. Put lemon drops around the top of the cake. Put gumdrops around the side of the cake.
    (You may make different patterns with the colorful gumdrops if you wish.)

Now your cat cake is finished!
I hope you enjoy eating it!

*Alex Whitney*
Alexandra Whitney

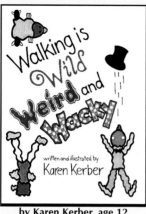

**by Karen Kerber, age 12**
St. Louis, Missouri
ISBN 0-933849-29-X    Full Color

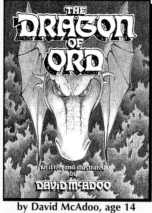

**by David McAdoo, age 14**
Springfield, Missouri
ISBN 0-933849-23-0    Inside Duotone

**by Amy Hagstrom, age 9**
Portola, California
ISBN 0-933849-15-X    Full Color

**by Isaac Whitlatch, age 11**
Casper, Wyoming
ISBN 0-933849-16-8    Full Color

**by Leslie Ann MacKeen, age 9**
Winston-Salem, North Carolina
ISBN 0-933849-19-2    Full Color

**by Elizabeth Haidle, age 13**
Beaverton, Oregon
ISBN 0-933849-20-6    Full Color

**by Heidi Salter, age 19**
Berkeley, California
ISBN 0-933849-21-4    Full Color

**by Lauren Peters, age 7**
Kansas City, Missouri
ISBN 0-933849-25-7    Full Color

**by Aruna Chandrasekhar, age 9**
Houston, Texas
ISBN 0-933849-33-8    Full Color

**by Anika Thomas, age 13**
Pittsburgh, Pennsylvania
ISBN 0-933849-34-6    Inside Two Colors

**by Cara Reichel, age 15**
Rome, Georgia
ISBN 0-933849-35-4    Inside Two Colors

**by Jonathan Kahn, age 9**
Richmond Heights, Ohio
ISBN 0-933849-36-2    Full Color

**by Benjamin Kendall, age 7**
State College, Pennsylvania
ISBN 0-933849-42-7    Full Color

**by Steven Shepard, age 13**
Great Falls, Virginia
ISBN 0-933849-43-5    Full Color

**by Travis Williams, age 16**
Sardis, B.C., Canada
ISBN 0-933849-44-3    Inside Two Colors

**by Dubravka Kolanović, age 1**
Savannah, Georgia
ISBN 0-933849-45-1    Full Color

# THE NATIONAL WRITTEN & ILLUSTRATED BY...AWARD WINNERS

**by Dav Pilkey, age 19**
Cleveland, Ohio
ISBN 0-933849-22-2    Full Color

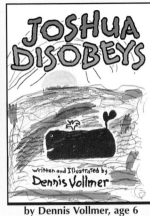

**by Dennis Vollmer, age 6**
Grove, Oklahoma
ISBN 0-933849-12-5    Full Color

**by Lisa Gross, age 12**
Santa Fe, New Mexico
ISBN 0-933849-13-3    Full Color

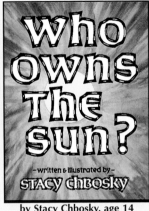

**by Stacy Chbosky, age 14**
Pittsburgh, Pennsylvania
ISBN 0-933849-14-1    Full Color

**by Michael Cain, age 11**
Annapolis, Maryland
ISBN 0-933849-26-5    Full Color

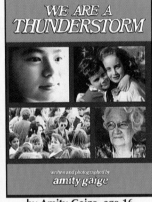

**by Amity Gaige, age 16**
Reading, Pennsylvania
ISBN 0-933849-27-3    Full Color

**by Adam Moore, age 9**
Broken Arrow, Oklahoma
ISBN 0-933849-24-9    Inside Duotone

**by Michael Aushenker, age 19**
Ithaca, New York
ISBN 0-933849-28-1    Full Color

**by Jayna Miller, age 19**
Zanesville, Ohio
ISBN 0-933849-37-0    Full Color

**by Bonnie-Alise Leggat, age 8**
Culpepper, Virginia
ISBN 0-933849-39-7    Full Color

**by Lisa Kirsten Butenhoff, age 13**
Woodbury, Minnesota
ISBN 0-933849-40-0    Full Color

**by Jennifer Brady, age 17**
Columbia, Missouri
ISBN 0-933849-41-9    Full Color

**by Amy Jones, age 17**
Shirley, Arkansas
ISBN 0-933849-46-X    Full Color

**by Shintaro Maeda, age 8**
Wichita, Kansas
ISBN 0-933849-51-6    Full Color

**by Miles MacGregor, age 12**
Phoenix, Arizona
ISBN 0-933849-52-4    Full Color

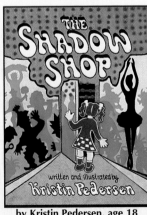

**by Kristin Pedersen, age 18**
Etobicoke, Ont., Canada
ISBN 0-933849-53-2    Full Color

Travis Williams
age 16

Anika D. Thomas
age 13

Isaac Whitlatch
age 11

Elizabeth Haidle
age 13

Miles MacGregor
age 12

Jayna Miller
age 19

Jonathan Kahn
age 9

Stacy Chbosky
age 14

David McAdoo
age 12

Amity Gaige
age 16

by Laura Hughes, age 8
Woonsocket, Rhode Island
ISBN 0-933849-57-5    Full Color

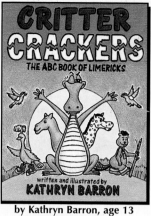

by Kathryn Barron, age 13
Emo, Ont., Canada
ISBN 0-933849-58-3    Full Color

by Taramesha Maniatty, age 15
Morrisville, Vermont
ISBN 0-933849-59-1    Full Color

by Lindsay Wolter, age 9
Cheshire, Connecticut
ISBN 0-933849-61-3    Full Color

by Anna Riphahn, age 13
Topeka, Kansas
ISBN 0-933849-62-1    Full Color

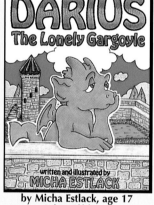

by Micha Estlack, age 17
Yukon, Oklahoma
ISBN 0-933849-63-X    Full Color

by Alexandra Whitney, age 8
Eugene, Oregon
ISBN 0-933849-64-8    Full Color

by Gillian McHale, age 10
Doylestown, Pennsylvania
ISBN 0-933849-65-6    Full Color

by Taylor Maw, age 17
Visalia, California
ISBN 0-933849-66-4    Full Color

## Books Created By Students For Students Are Amazing.

That's true!  BOOKS FOR STUDENT BY STUDENTS® are absolutely amazing.  They dazzle. They astound.  They inform.  And they delight.

All the stories are beautifully, thoughtfully, and cleverly written.  And the illustration are outstanding displays of artistic talents and skills.

Some of the books are so funny, they will make you laugh aloud.  And some of th books are so touching, they will bring tears to your eyes.

The books do all the things that really good books do because they really are goo books.  When you see these exceptional books, you are bound to be proud of the stu dents who created them.  And you will be thrilled to share them with your students.

These are important books, too.  Not only do they inform and entertain, but they also hav the power to motivate and inspire your students to write and illustrate their own books.

**Kewaskum Public Library**
206 First Street, Box 38
Kewaskum, WI 53040-0038
(414) 626-4312